PIXEL ART

make
believe
ideas

Use the pixels to create incredible art and cool designs.
Choose an image, then copy it onto the cover board.

The art in the book is broken down into three levels.
Level 1 uses the least pixels; level 3 uses the most.

Once you've mastered the art of picture creation,
step up to the PIXEL ART Challenges.

CHALLENGE 1: Go against the clock

Time how long it takes you to complete an image,
then challenge yourself to recreate it in half the time.

Go head-to-head with a friend for a PIXEL ART showdown!
Who can complete a picture in the fastest time?

Can you recreate a picture in under a minute?

CHALLENGE 2: Memory challenge

Stare at an image for one minute, then try to recreate it from memory only. Start with a level one image, and work your way up.

CHALLENGE 3: Go create!

Use the grid on the back of each image to make your own PIXEL ART design, then recreate it on the cover board.

Challenge yourself and your friends to create different objects.

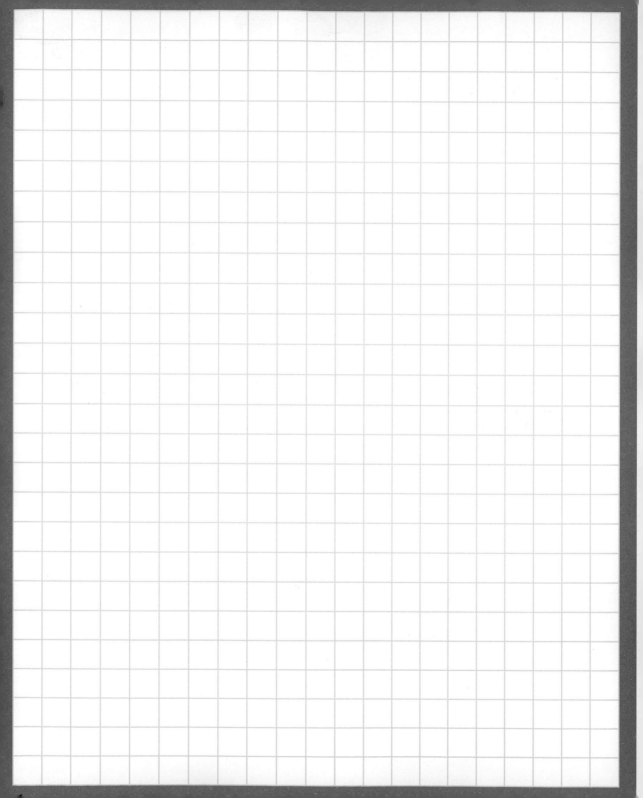

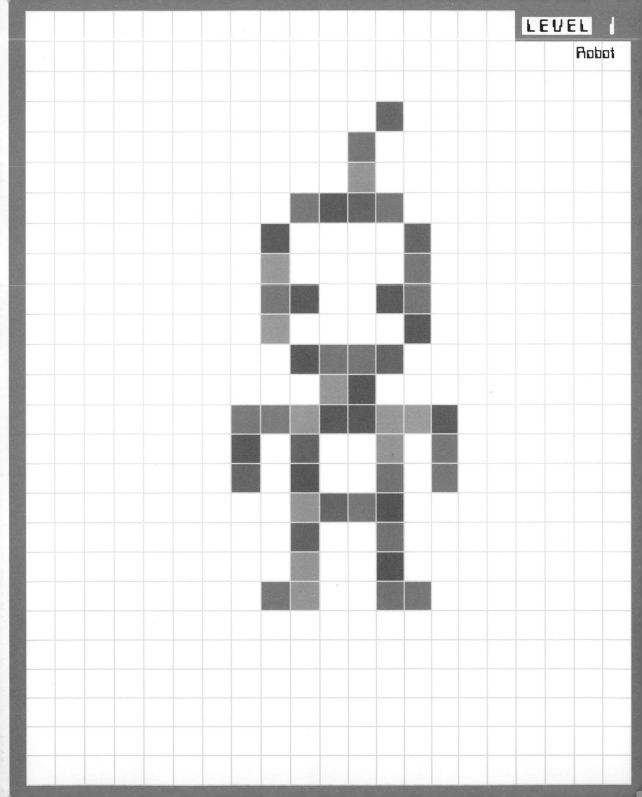

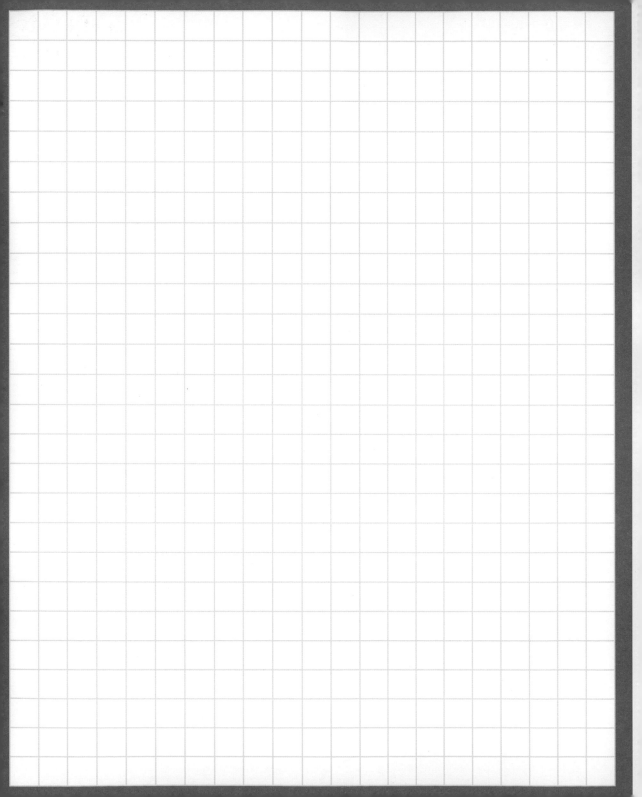

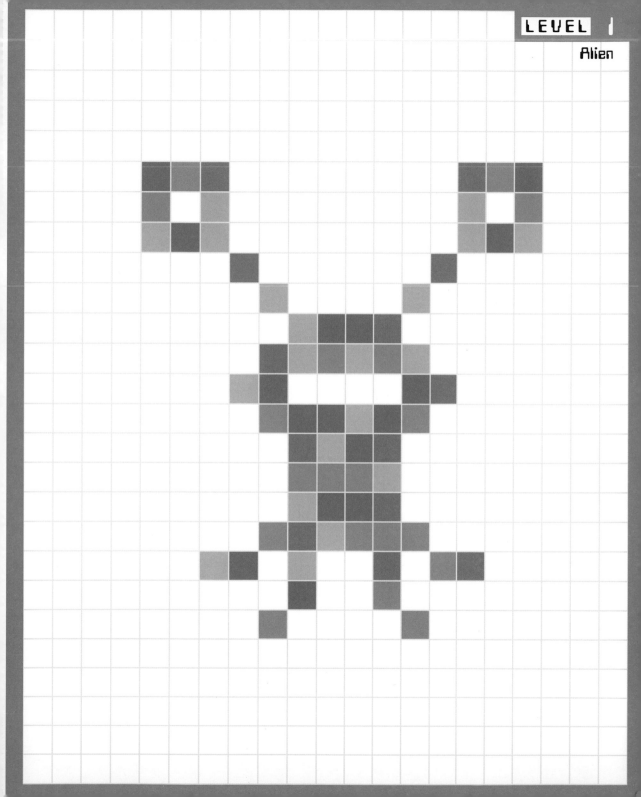

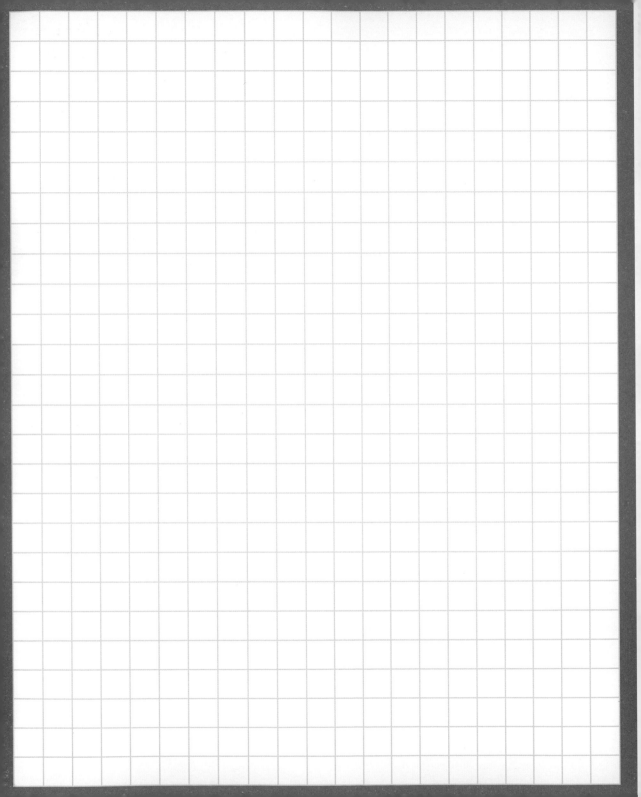

Pac-Man

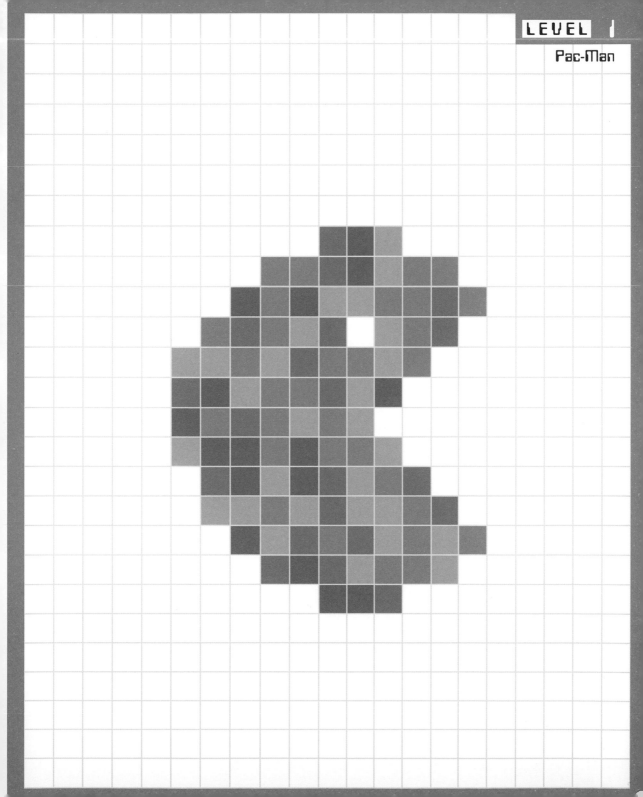

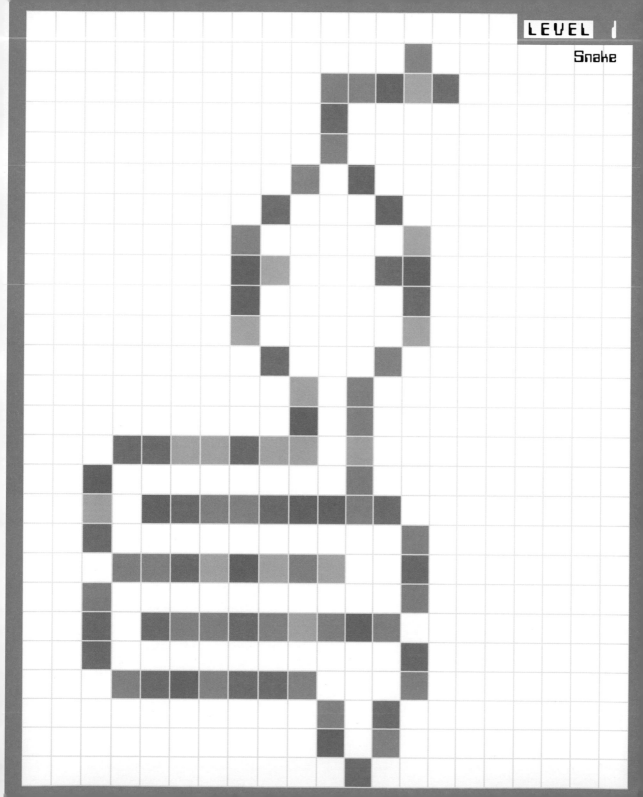

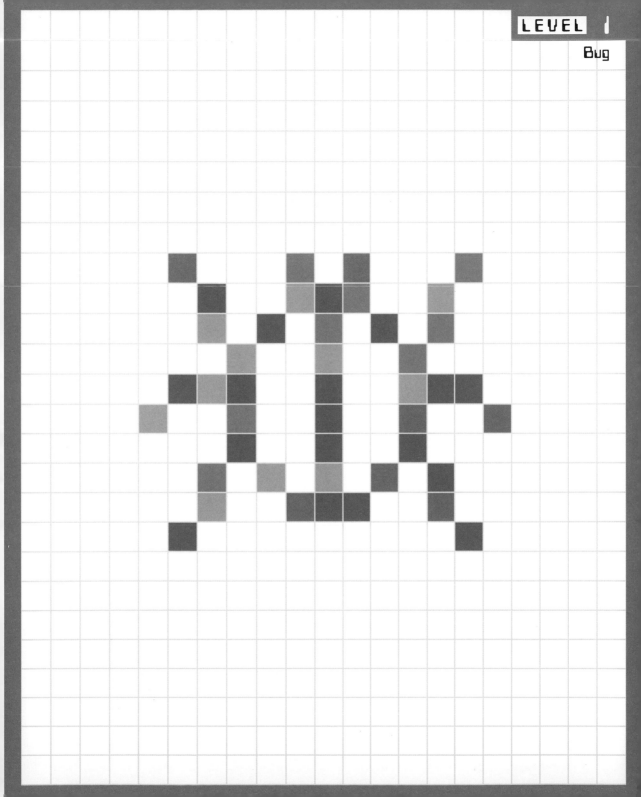

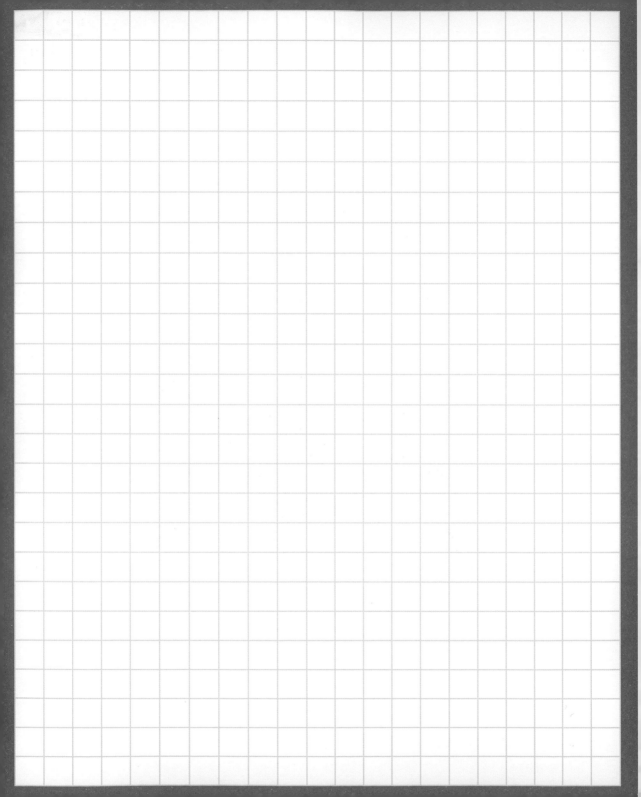

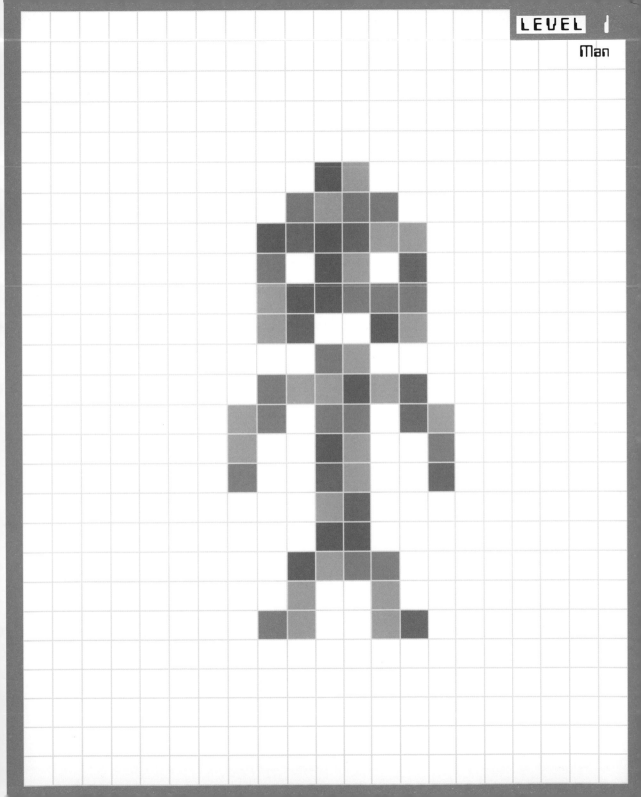

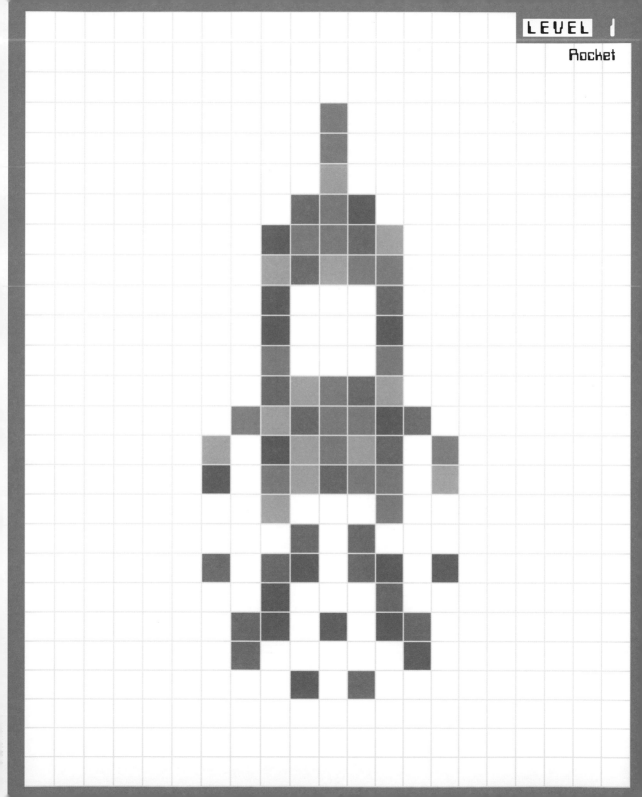

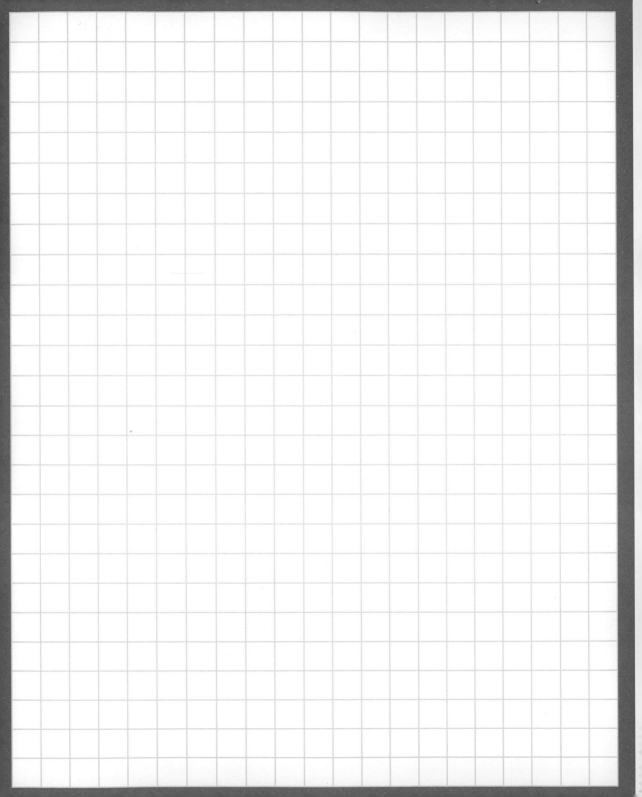

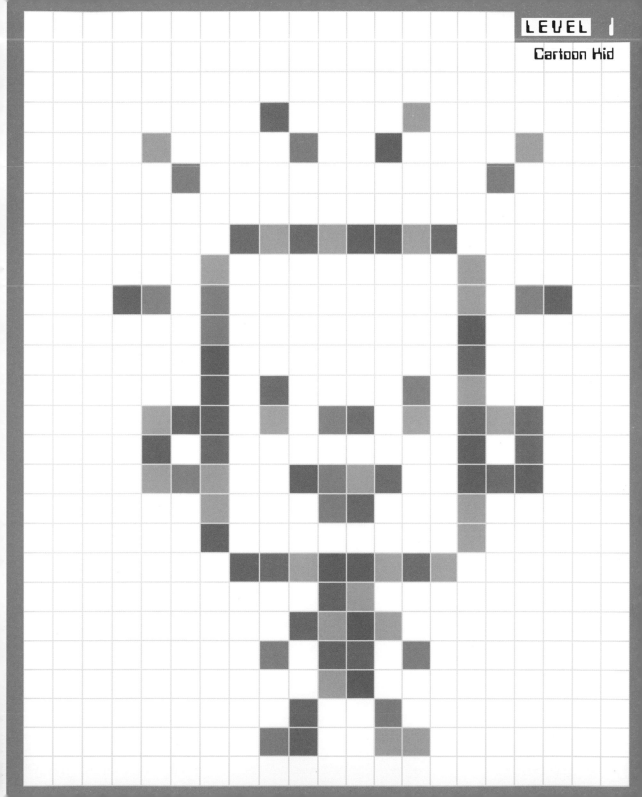

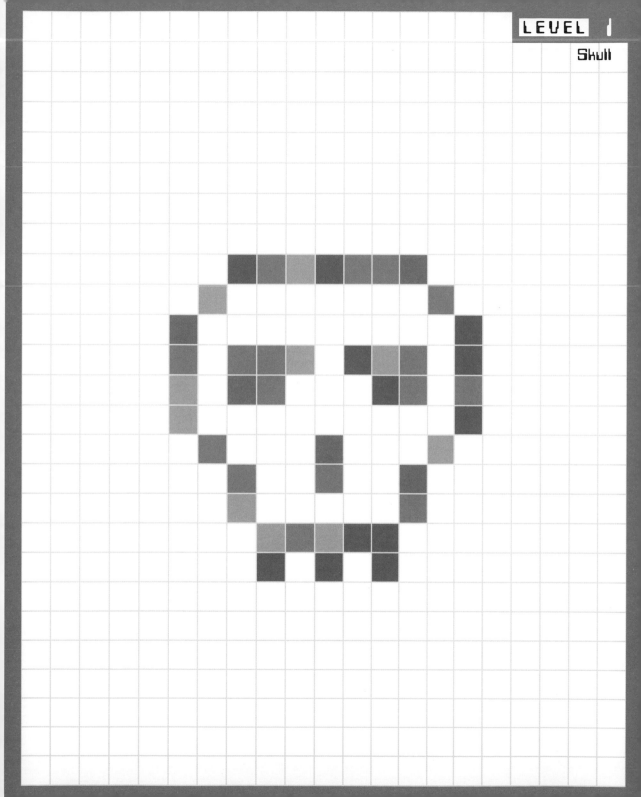

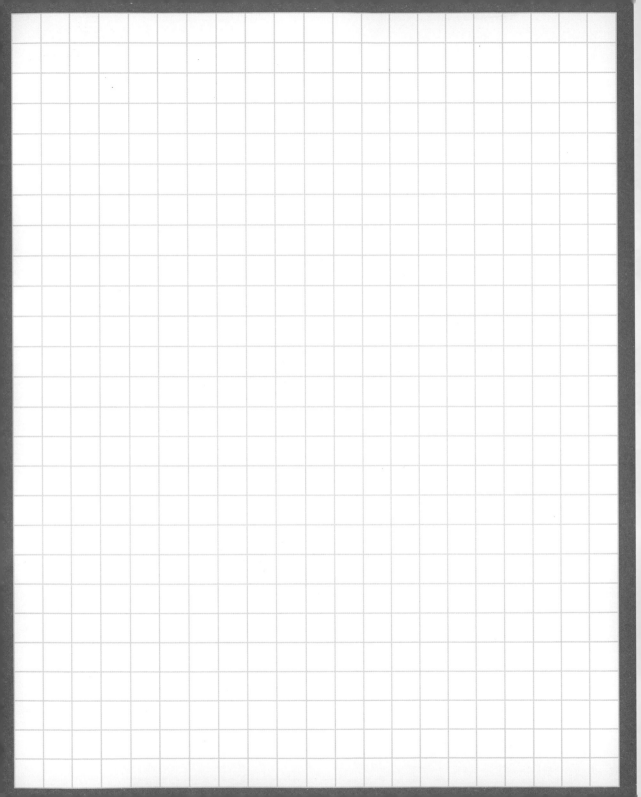

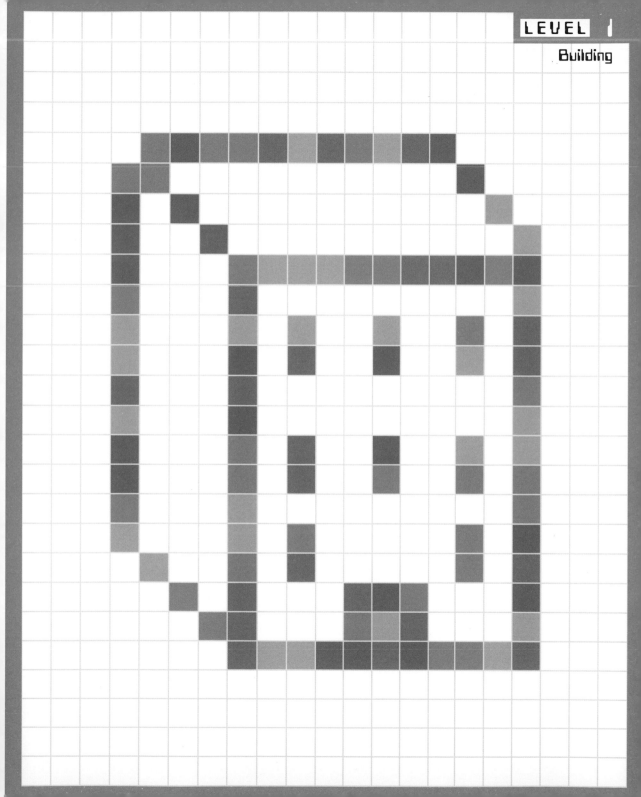

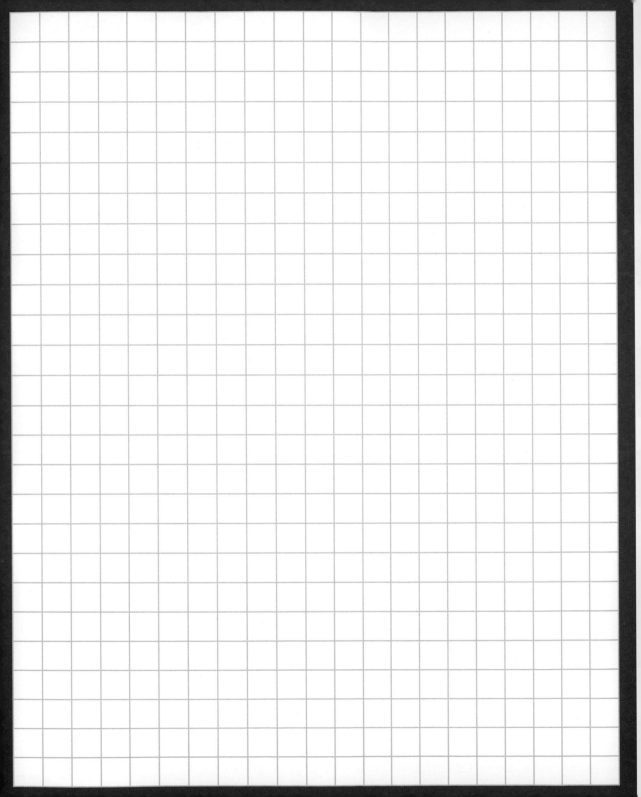

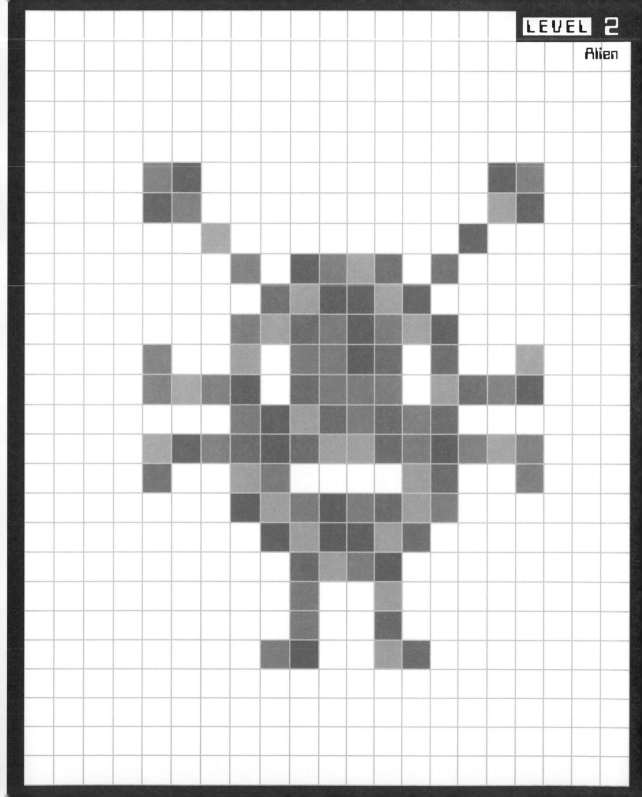

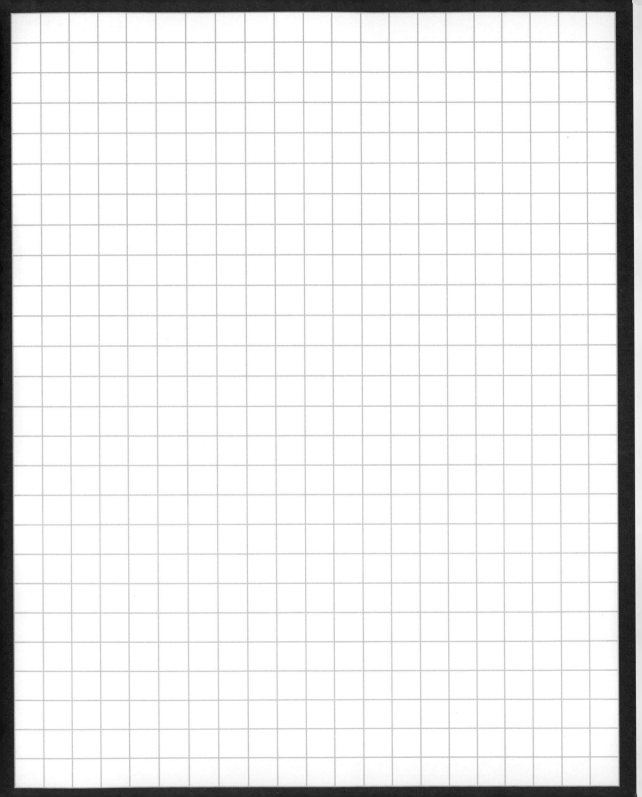

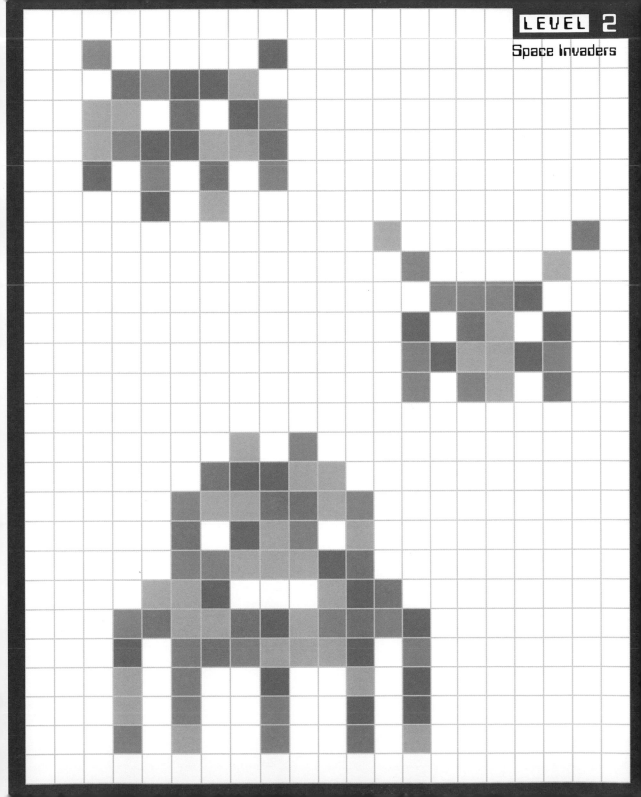

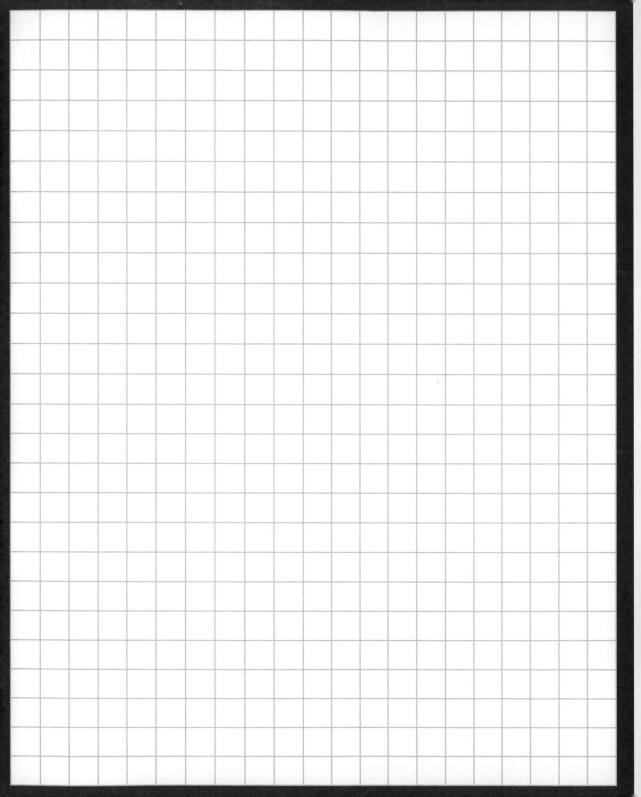

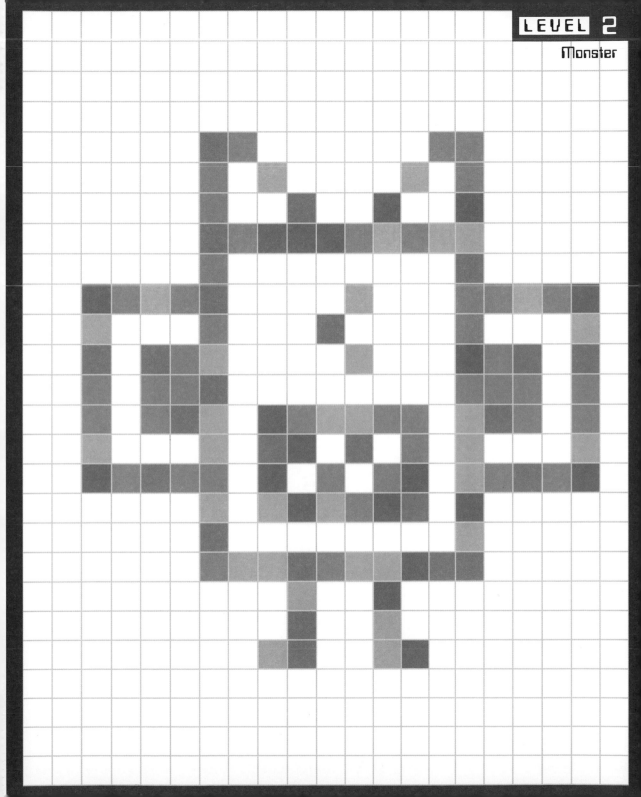

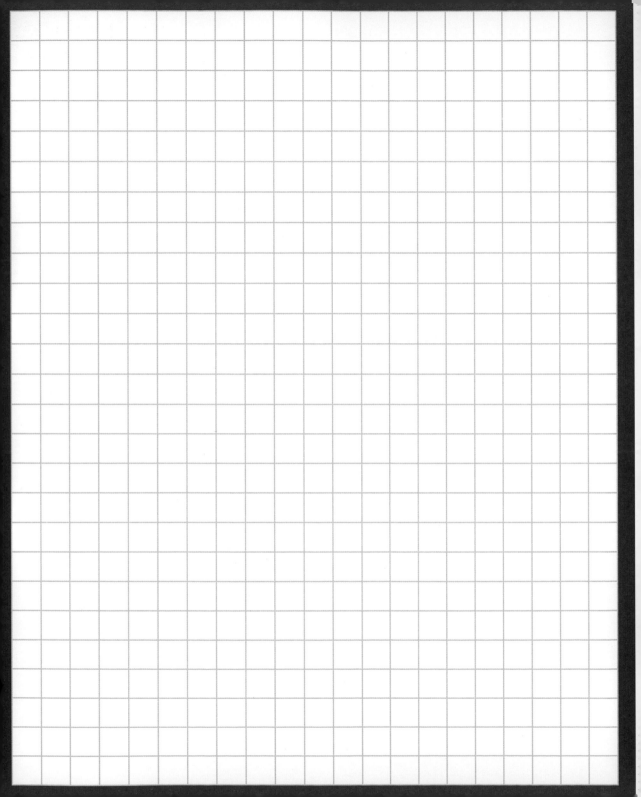

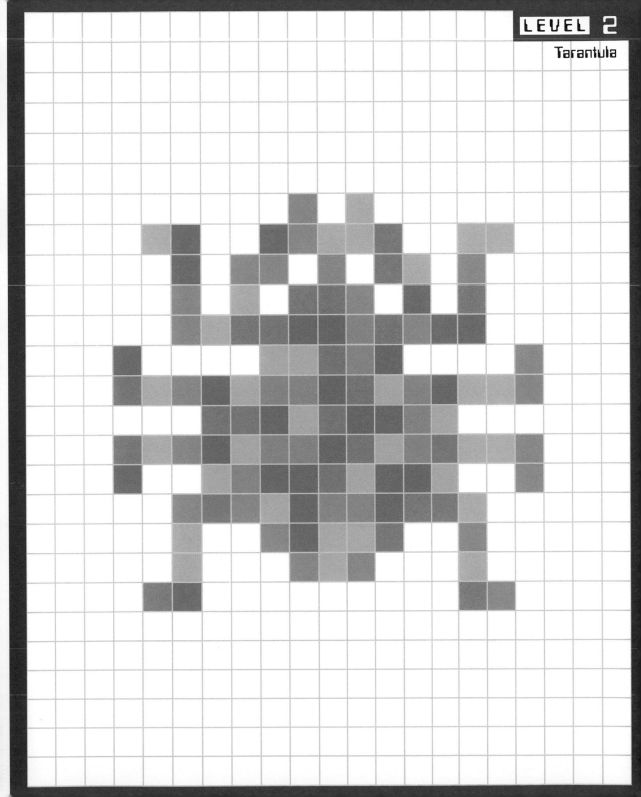

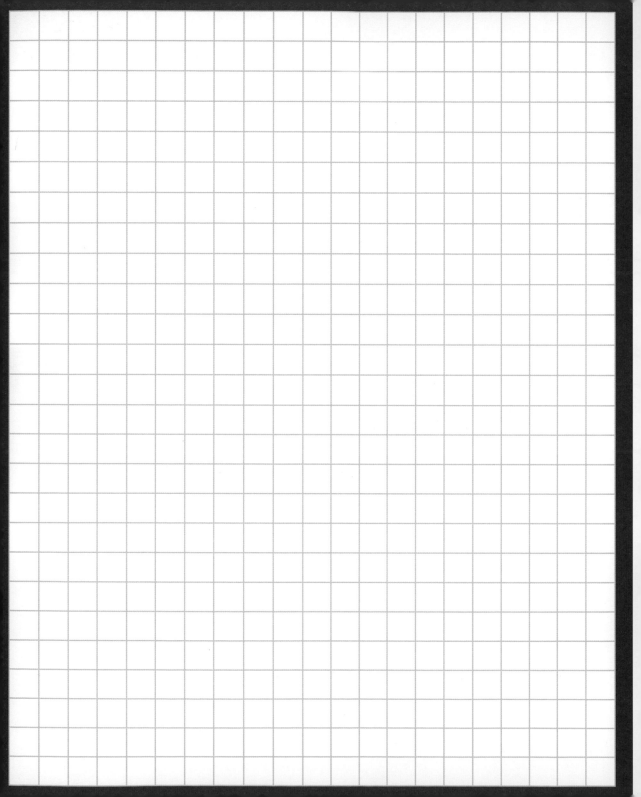

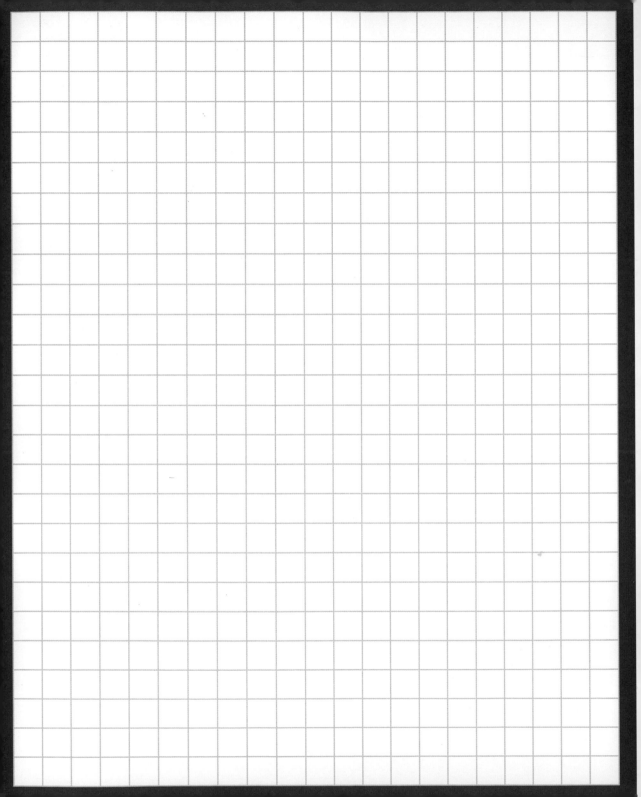

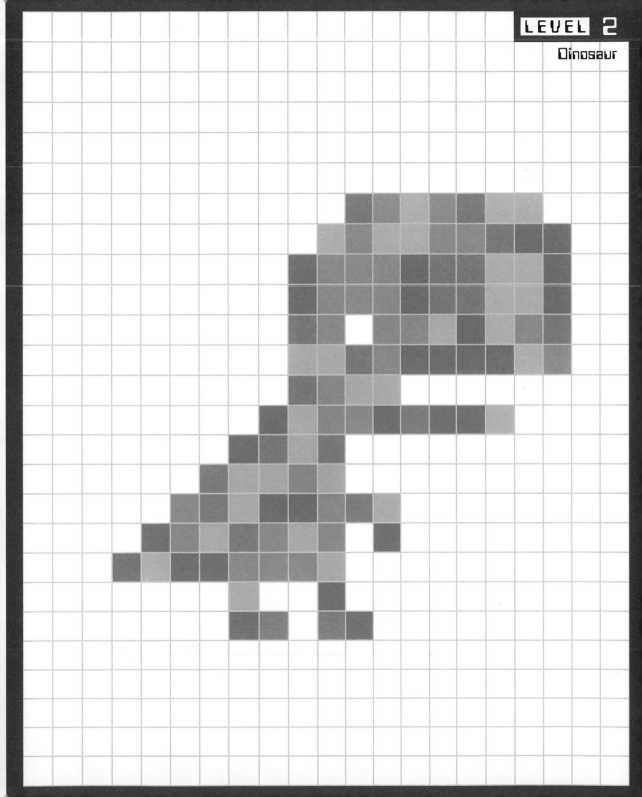

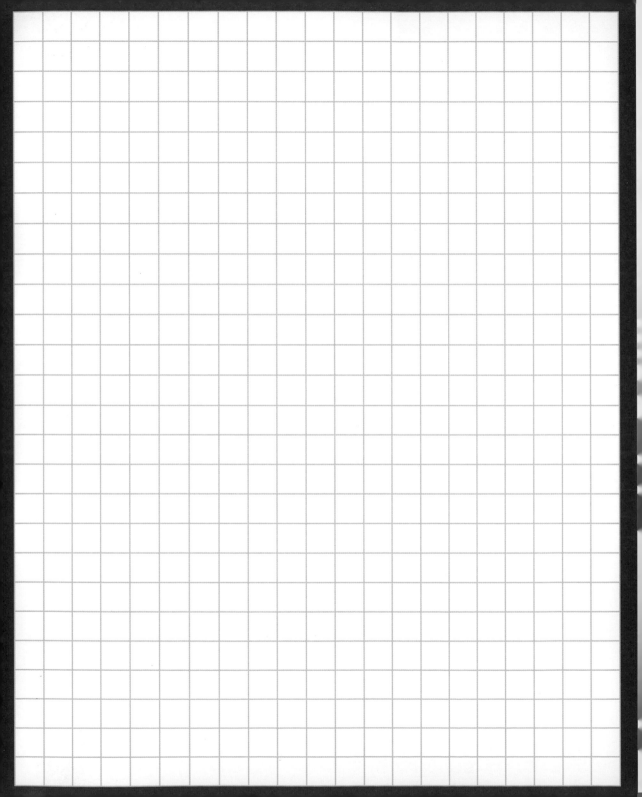

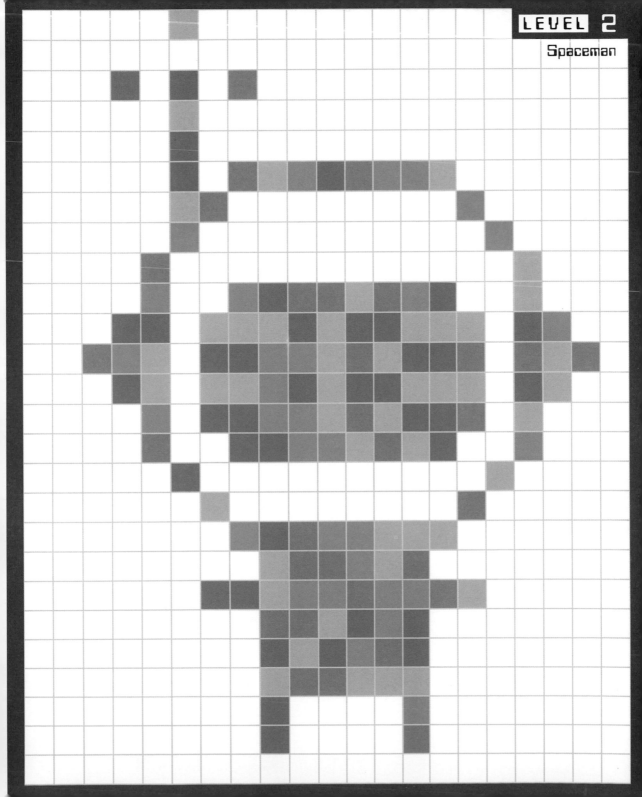

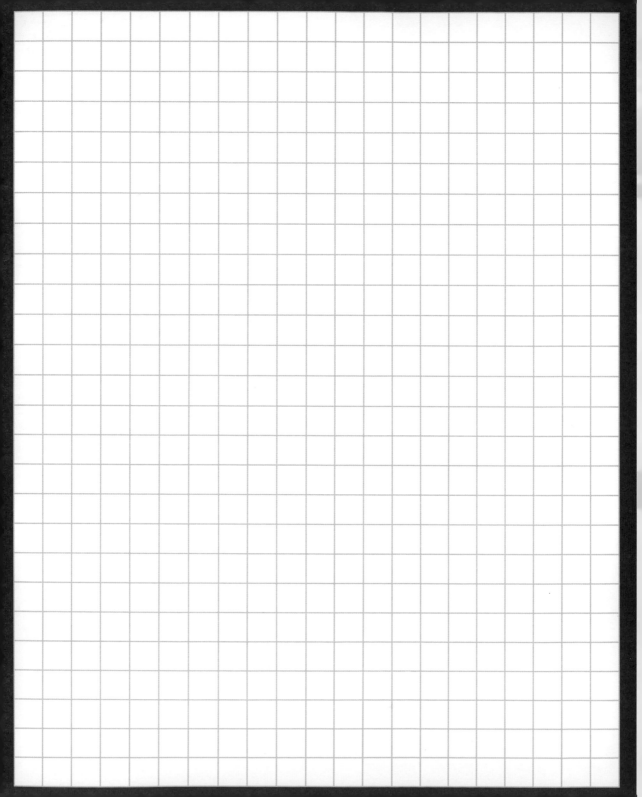

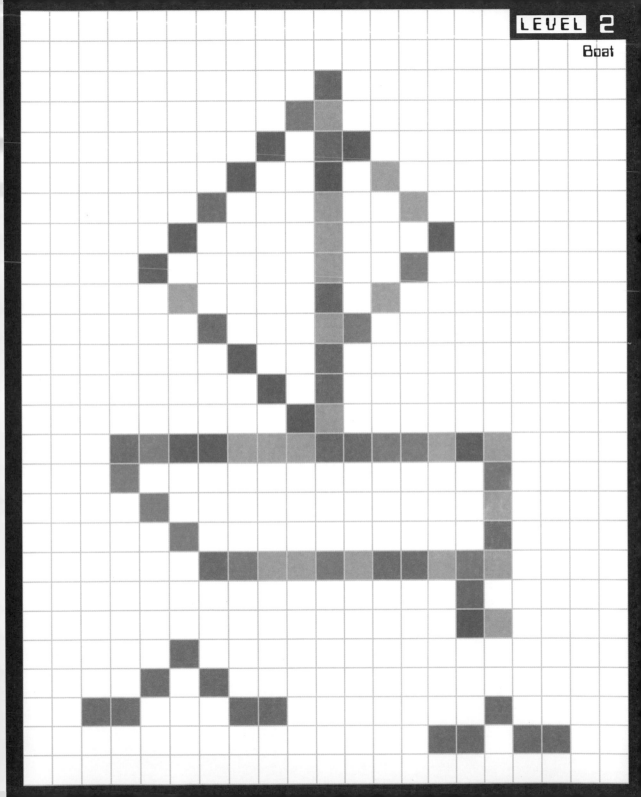

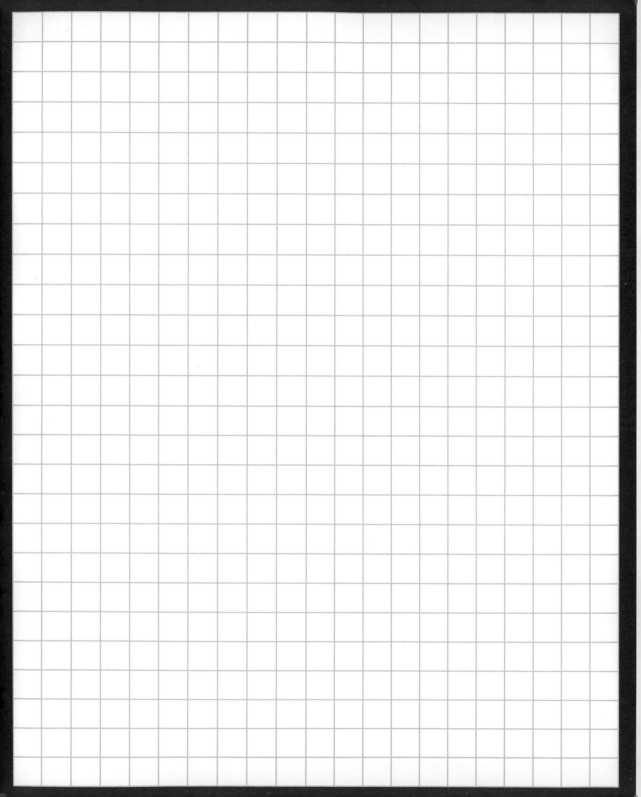

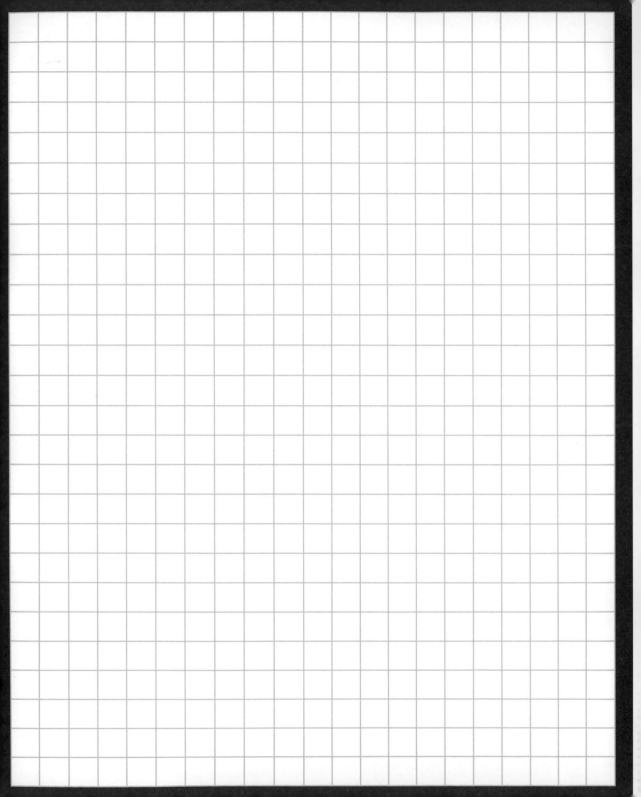

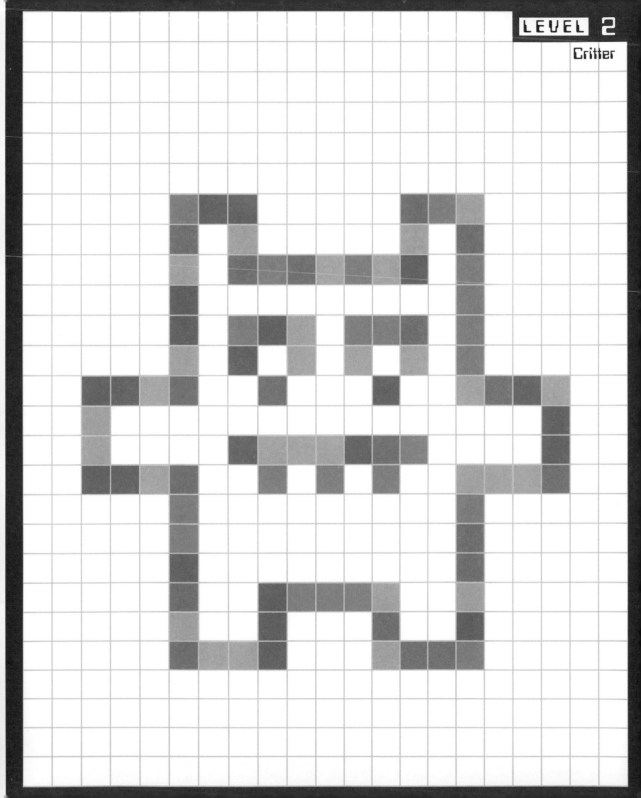

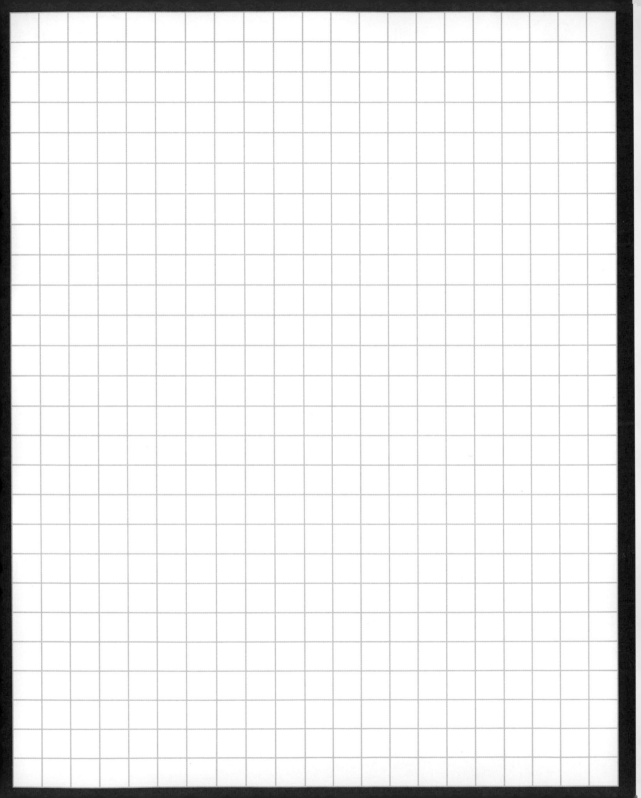

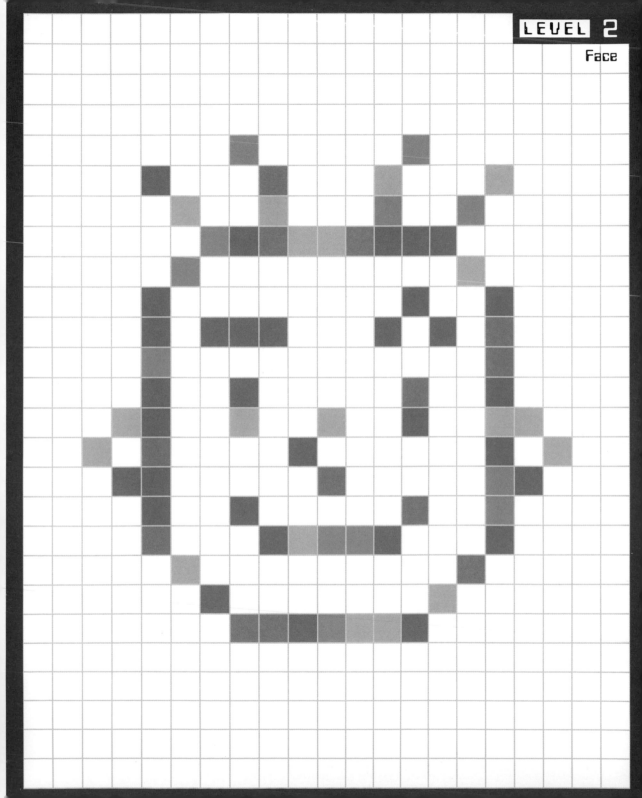

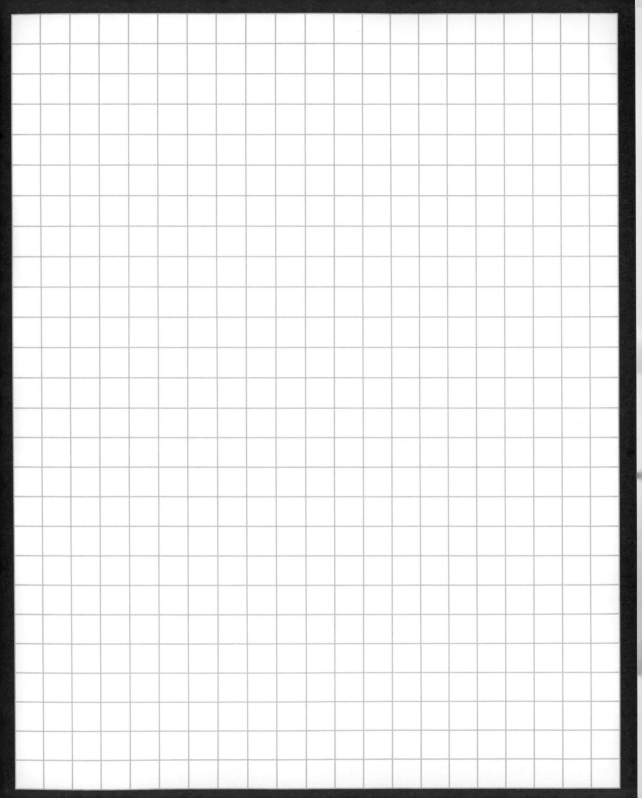

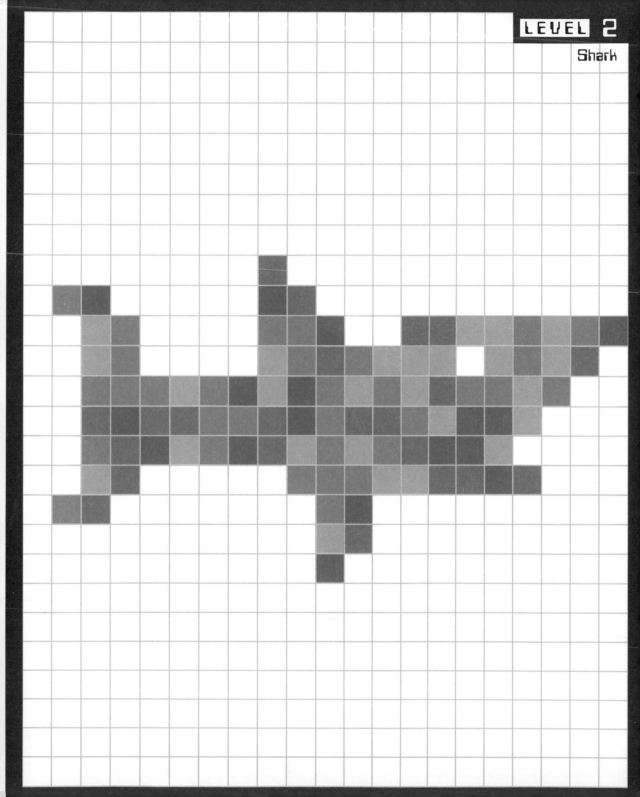

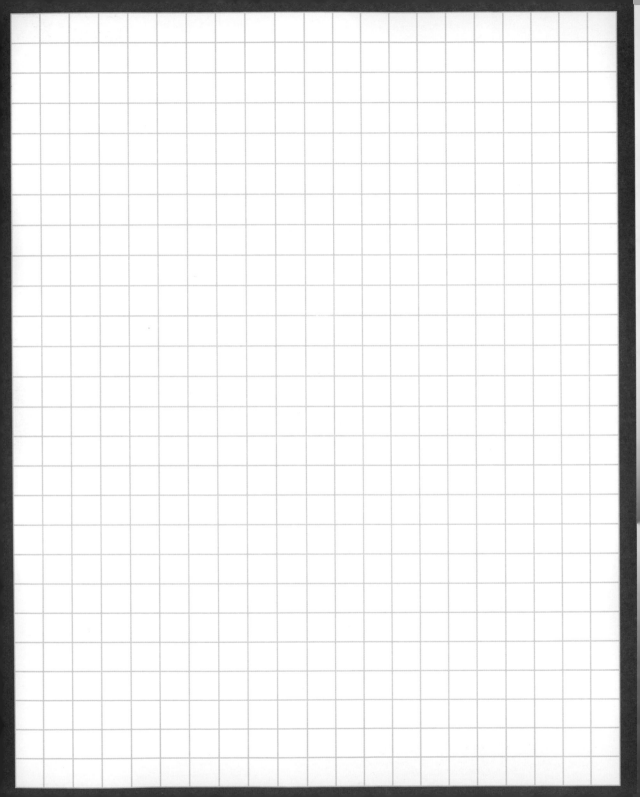

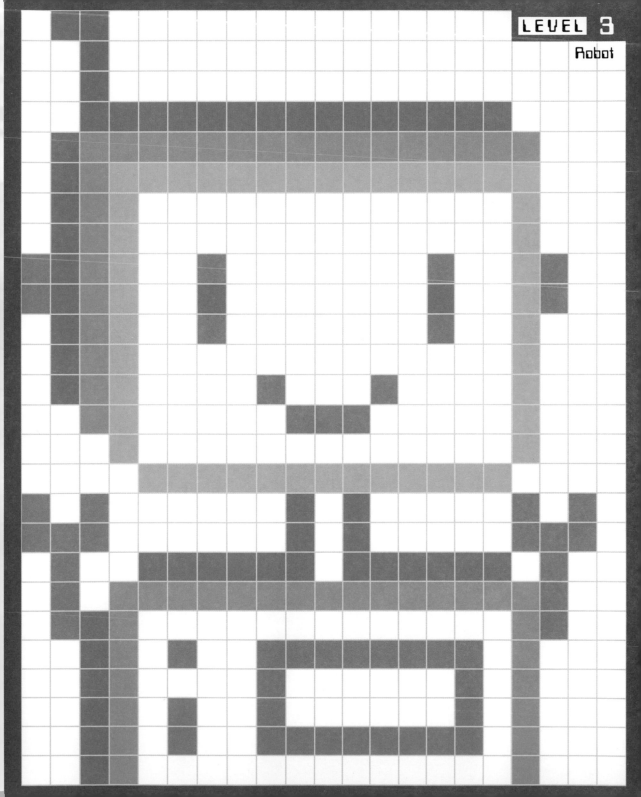

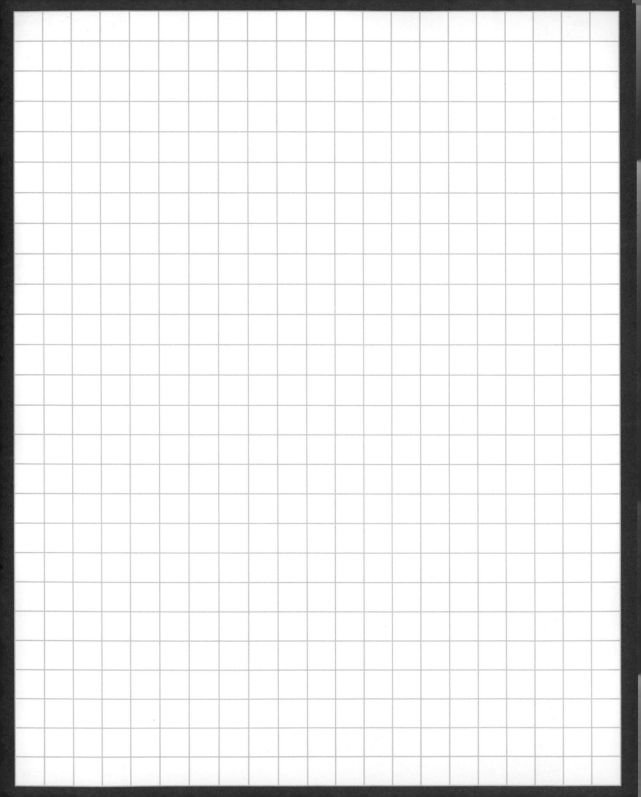

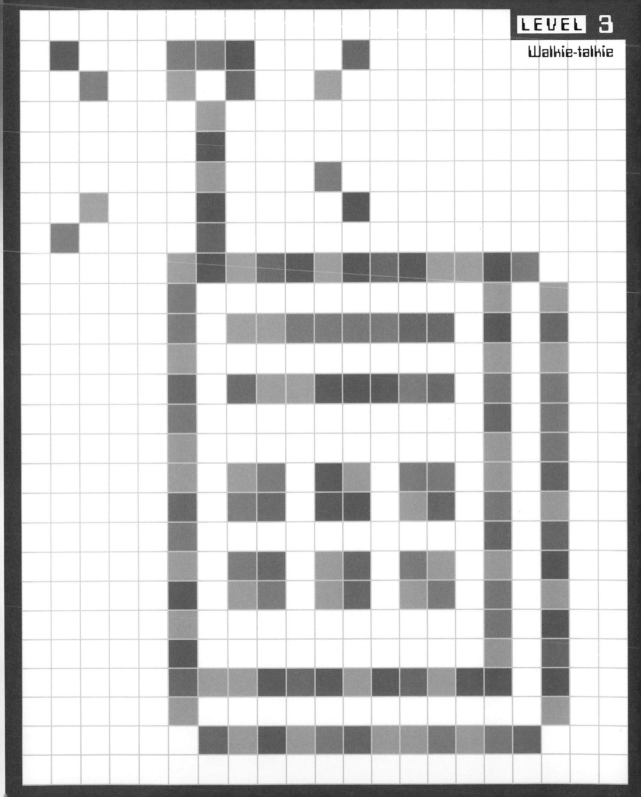

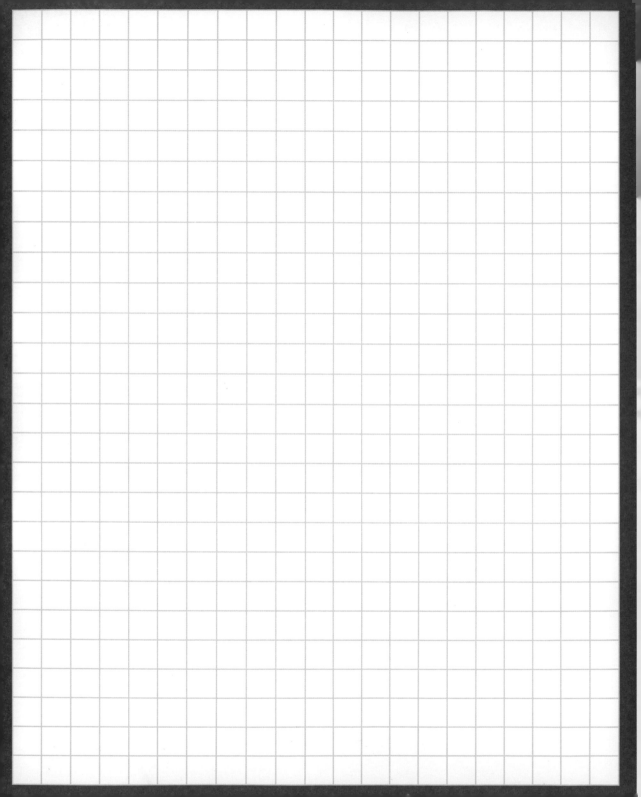

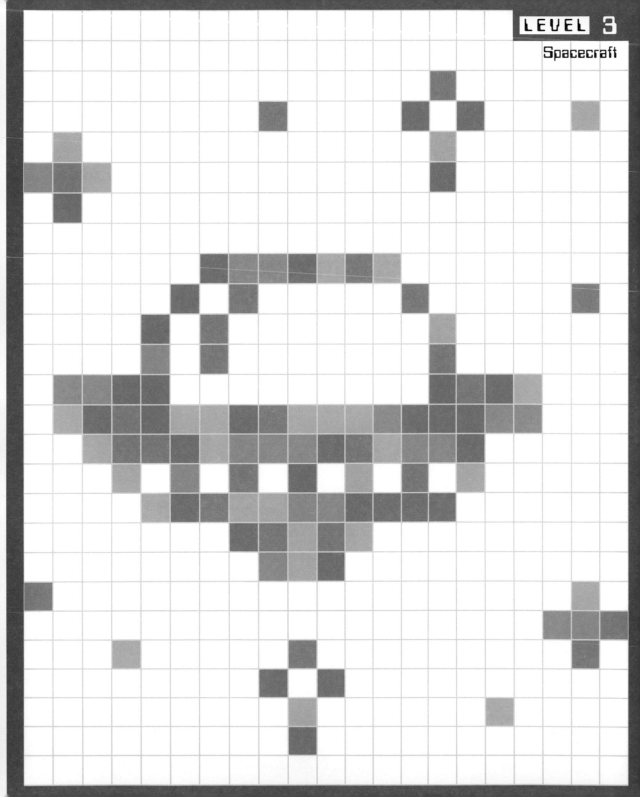

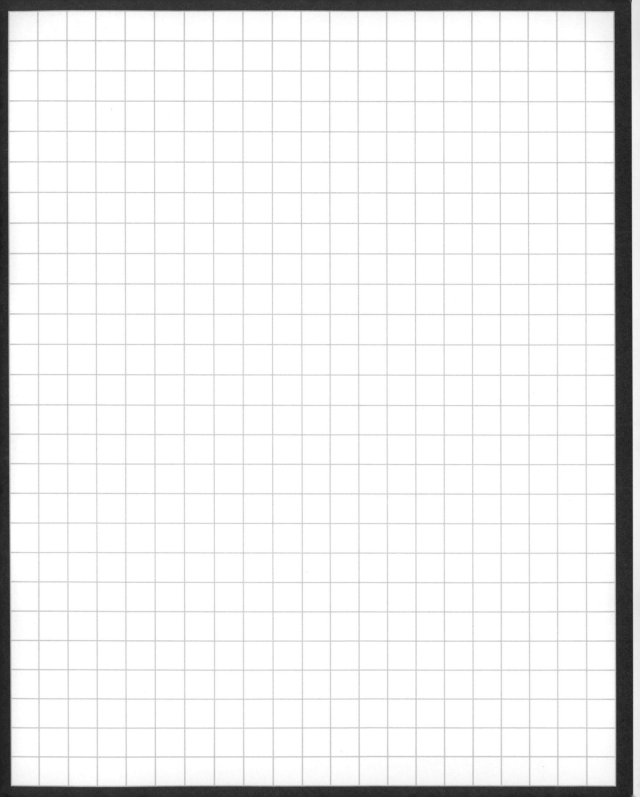

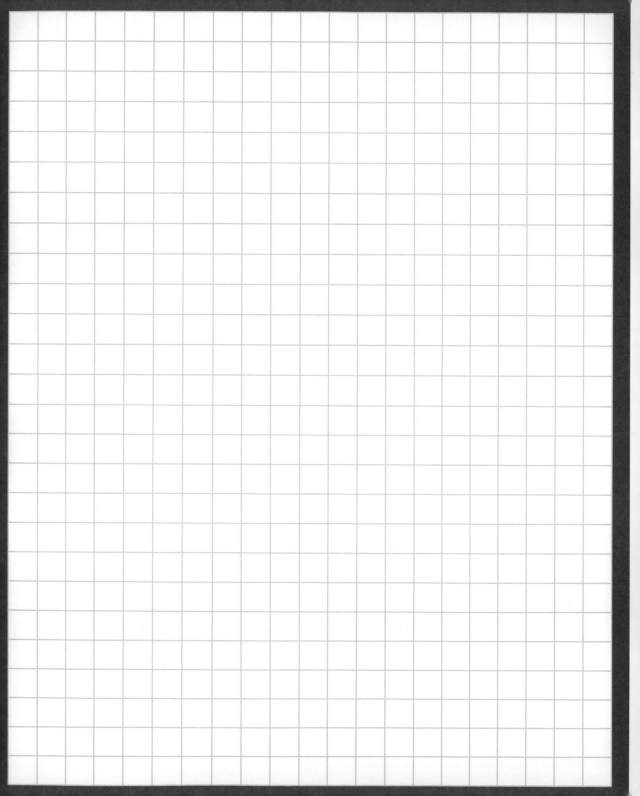

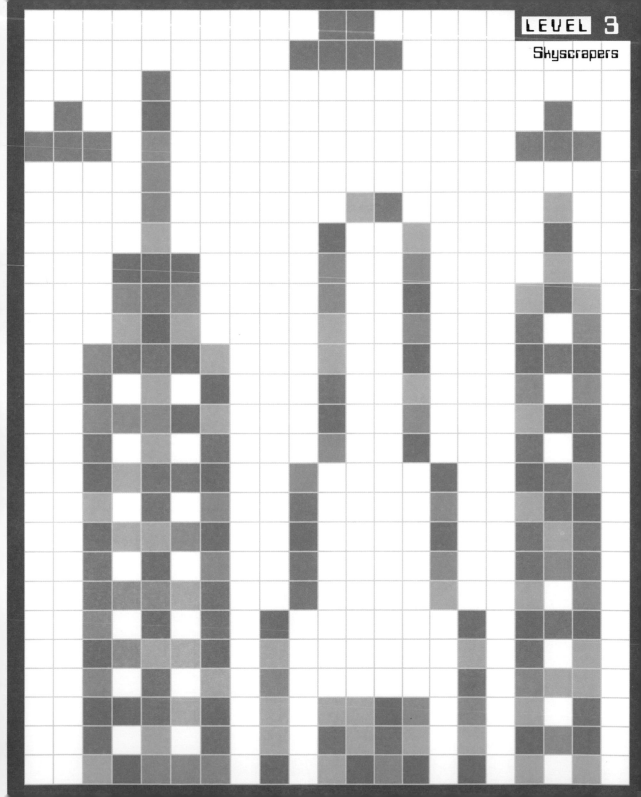

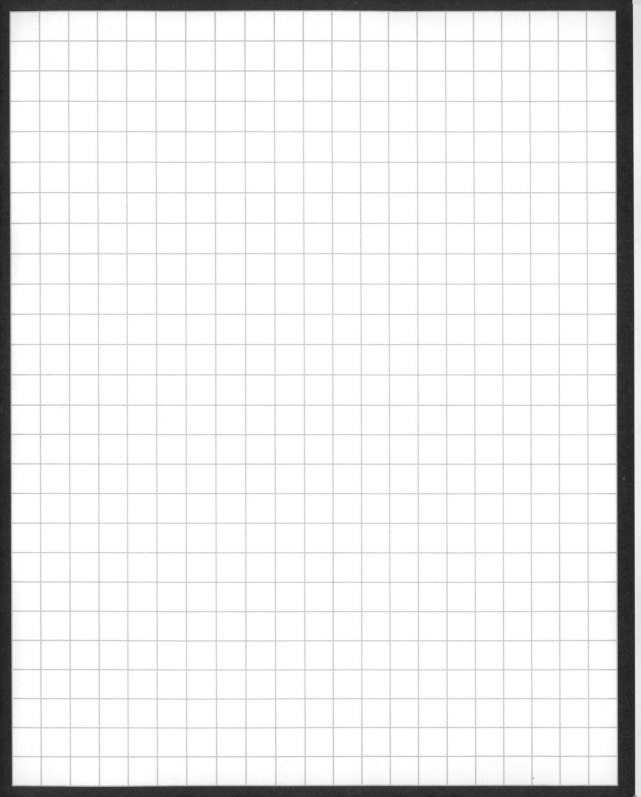

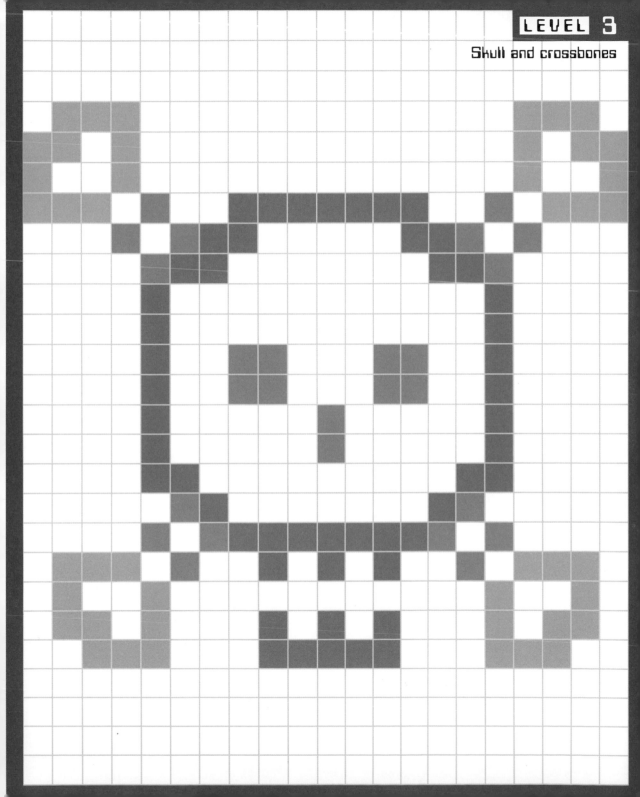

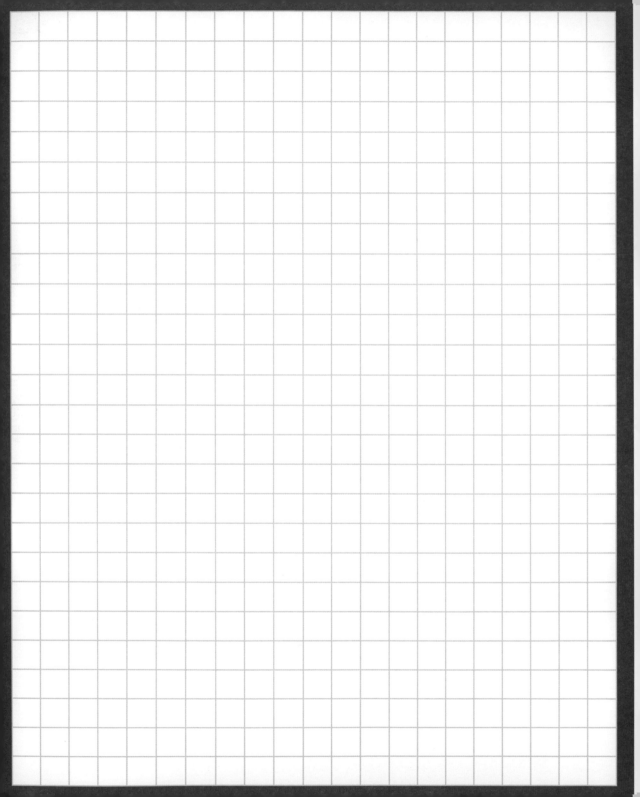

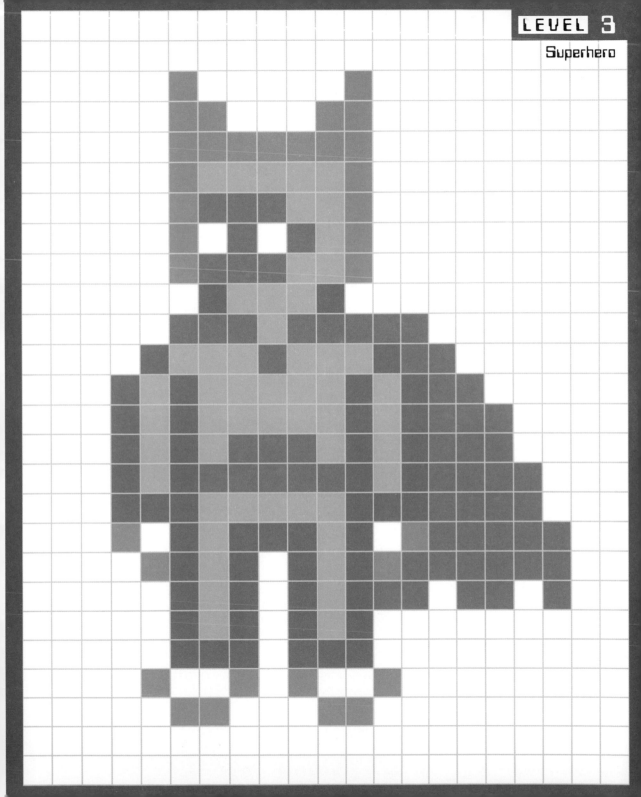

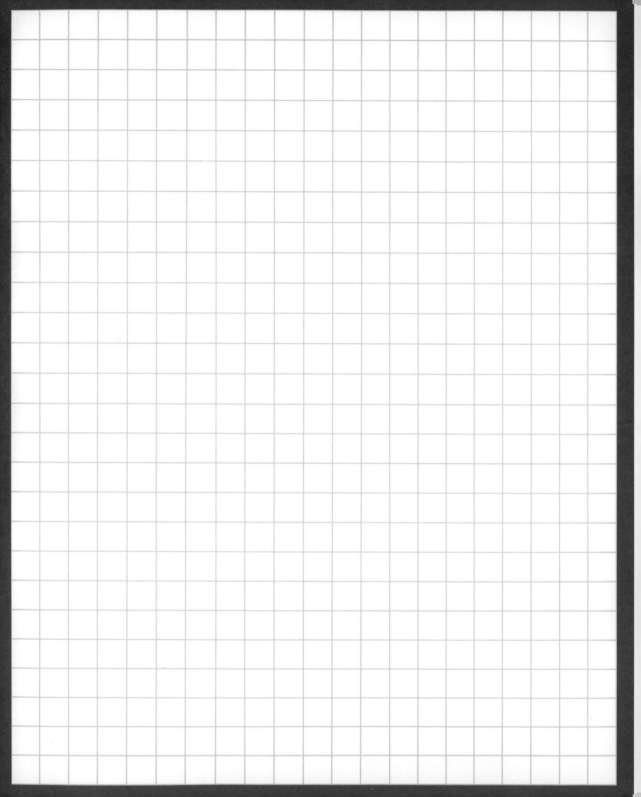

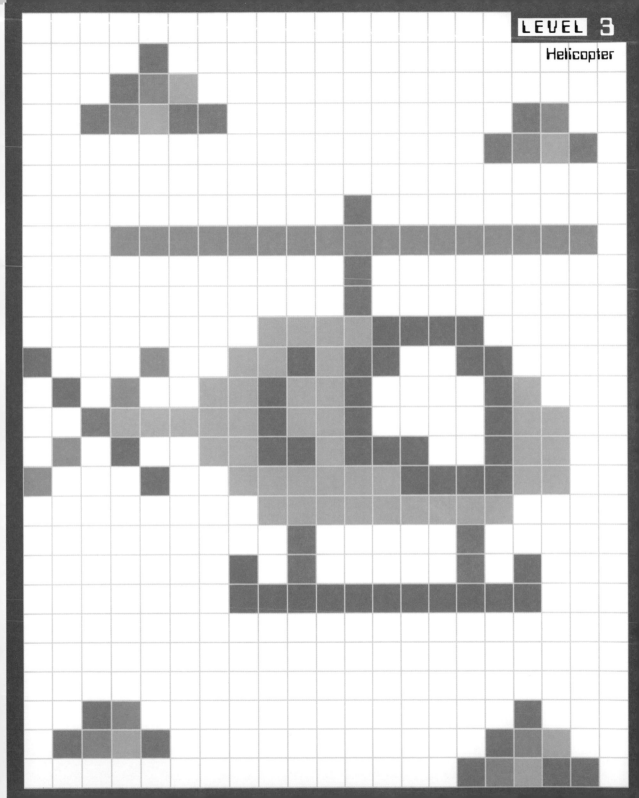

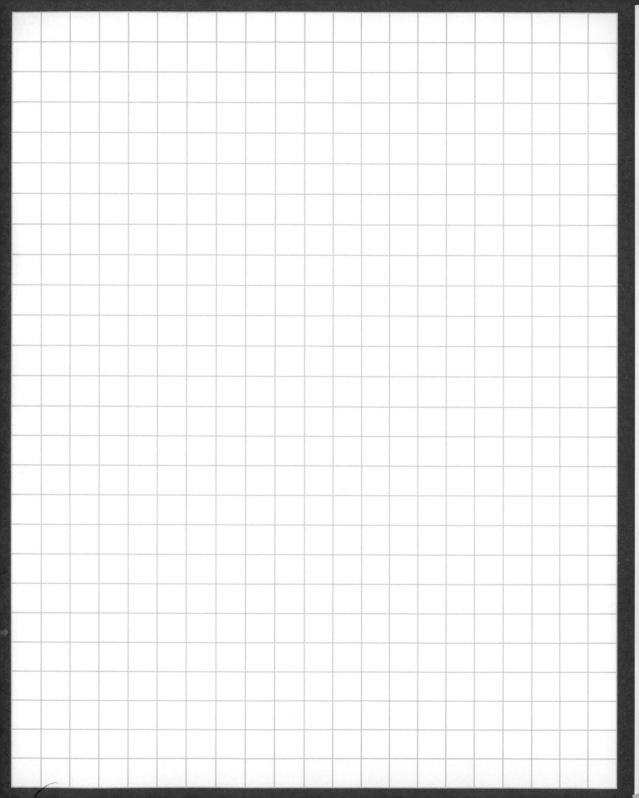

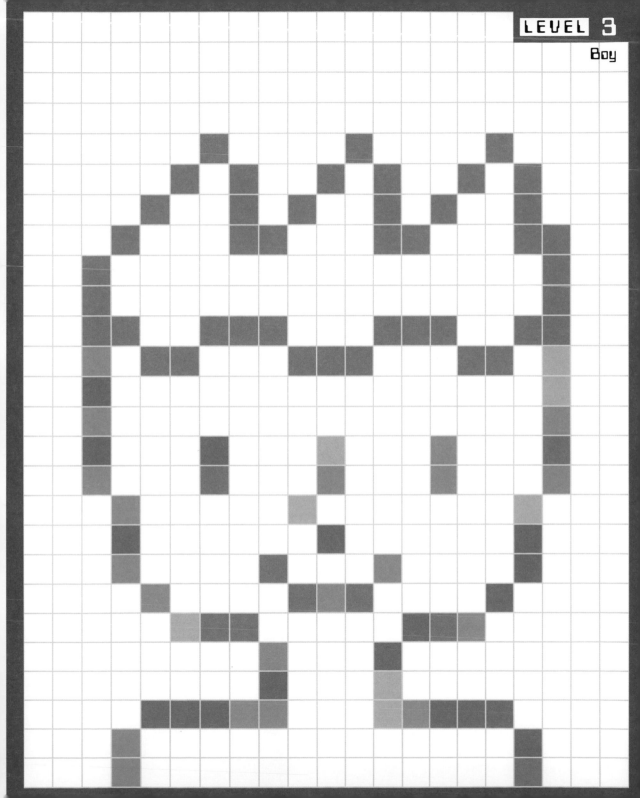

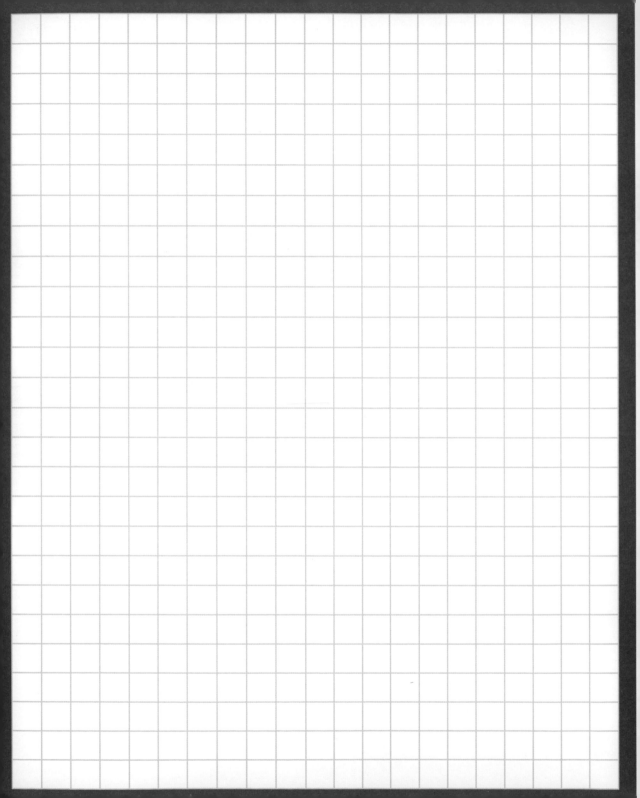

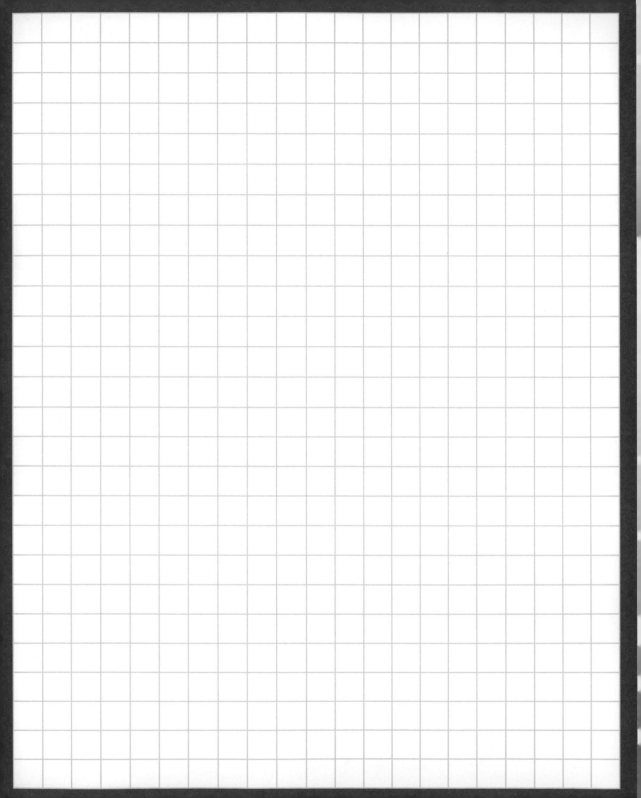

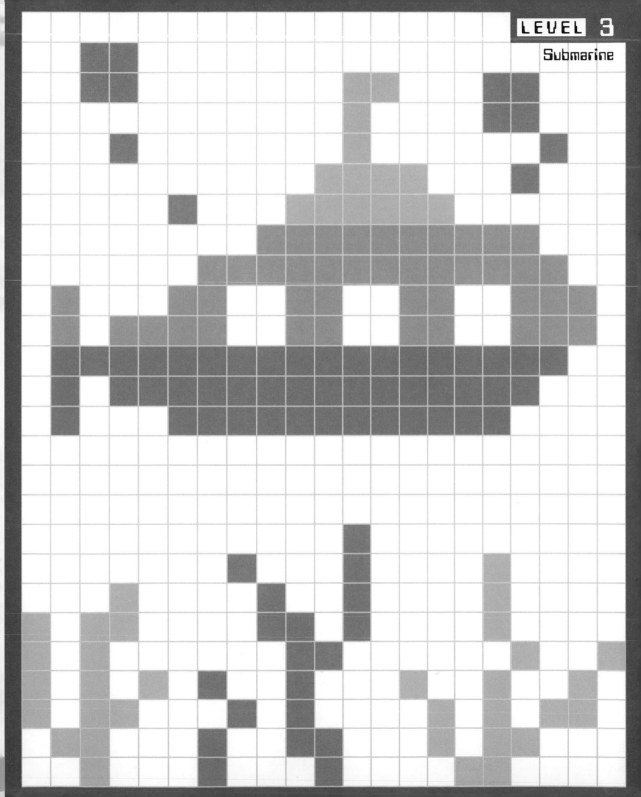

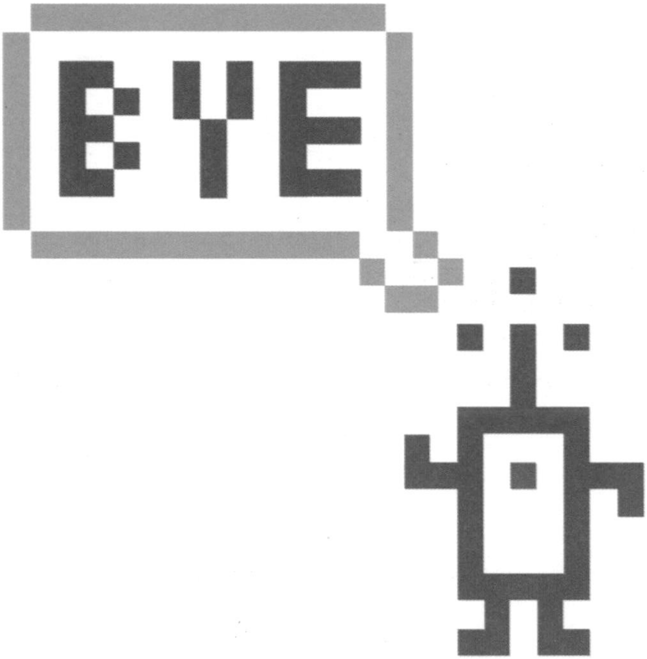
BYE